The Deadly Boutique
PAUL MAGRS

Proudly published by Snowbooks Ltd
ISBN 978-1-913525-35-4
Copyright © 2025 Paul Magrs
Cover art by Paul Magrs
Typeset by Emma Barnes in LATEX
British Library Cataloguing in Publication Data.
A catalogue record for this book is available from the British Library.

Read the whole Brenda and Effie Series:

The Deadly Boutique

I love it here.

It's the only place I could have settled down. I've never found a town like it, never in my long, long life.

My name is Brenda. Hello!

Since the beginning of summer I have lived here, deliciously inconspicuous: just one more Bed and Breakfast lady in a resort that teems with Bed and Breakfasts. Here, the streets are narrow and intricate; the rooftops are ramshackle and the wind is biting. The sea gulls are as big as Yorkshire terriers and, for a good nine months of the year this town is steeped in a thick sea mist... and that's probably a good thing.

There are things here that you don't necessarily want to see.

Keep your head down, Brenda. That's what I tell myself. Fry those sausages and eggs and bacon. Make those beds. Be welcoming. Be at home.

Now it is autumn. I have settled into the gloomy, doom-laden, chintzy Gothic atmosphere of this place.

And I love it.

§

I am a woman of a certain age who is ready to settle down. In the past I have had to pick myself up, time and again, and reinvent my life from scratch.

Now I want a quiet life.

I have known adversity and disaster and dodgy relationships. I have moved around from place to place, all over these islands. Sometimes I have even had to go on the run.

Now I want a quiet life. A respectable life.

I have no family. No ties.

I want to look after others.

What I want to do is keep everything immaculate and just so, making sure that the breakfasts and teas are on time and that the rooms are exact with the correct number of towels and flannels and little bars of soap. My guests are quite particular. My establishment attracts a certain class of person, I would say, though I am not a snob.

My friend Effie, who owns the junk shop next door, is a bit lah-de-dah and she says that I am obsessed with getting things right for my guests. She used the word 'mania'. She says no one else running a B+B in this town goes to the same trouble. For all her airs and graces, Effie is a bit slapdash about her own place.

She's the arty type. She's very literary. The only books I have are the Bible and Milton and Shelley, of course. I make sure there are copies in every one of my three rooms, in the drawer of the bedside cabinets. And two fresh bath towels laid out, two flannels for every basin, and the curtains are always opened exactly a foot wide, to let enough sunshine in, but not so much as to let the room look bleak. Effie says I fuss, but it's like someone once said, God is in the details.

But don't get me on the subject of God. Effie tried once and I had to get her to stop. She understands now that my God and her God are not quite the same. That was as far as the conversation went. Effie is a good friend to me, but like everyone else in Whitby, she knows nothing about my past.

No one living knows about my past.

I always wanted pretty things. I wanted chintz sofas and chairs, and nicely patterned curtains in light fabrics. I wanted colourful, dainty crockery. And I wanted to please people. To serve them tasty, wholesome, well-cooked food. I've got a craze for cleaning. I wait until the guests go out in the mornings, and leave their rooms all a-tumble, strewn with seaside holiday bric-a-brac. And then I creep in, clutching cloths and yellow dusters and a tin of baking soda. I crouch in bath tubs and sprinkle on the powder and I scour to my heart's content. Everything has to shine.

My livelihood depends upon the excellence of my establishment.

Despite everything, I am, in the end, more or less, a self-made woman.

§

Mondays I take my afternoon off.

Effie and I stroll along the Prom, up the hill, to the Christmas Hotel for afternoon tea. It isn't the swishest of hotels, as Effie says. But I like it. I like its deep, cavernous interior and its ancient, unchanging clientele. I love to sit in the conservatory at the front, at our usual table, overlooking the craggy, inhospitable bay. I like to sip too-hot tea and crumble biscuits and stare at the jet black cliffs and the ruined abbey and the fathomless sky.

Effie grumbles and moans, of course. As I say, she puts on airs, and wishes she was somewhere altogether nicer. Yet she has been coming here since she was a child. She has lived here all her life and inherited the house and all her belongings from her family, which has always been rooted here. I envy her that much. She could no more think about leaving this town and her routinized days than she could suddenly sprout a second head.

She's neat and slim, Effie. In a pale grey woollen suit, little ruffles round the neck of her lilac blouse.

She takes a twist of lemon in her tea and her mouth is pursed much of the time. Appraising. Watchful.

This Monday afternoon her eyes were narrowed as she gazed around the conservatory of the Christmas Hotel. Neither of us bothered to comment on the party hats the decrepit hotel guests wore, or the crackers they struggled feebly to pull or the dusty swags of vulgar tinsel strewn everywhere. This is a hotel frozen forever on the cusp of Christmas Eve. That is its selling point, its gimmick, and it is the way its eccentric proprietress liked it to be.

So it wasn't the festive lavishness that was attracting Effie's frown of intrigue.

She was staring at our waitress, Jessie, who invariably served us our afternoon tea here on Mondays. She was approaching with the tea trolley and its usual freight of gleaming, tinkling china; squashy cakes, mounds of golden cream, and precise geometrical arrangements of egg and cress sandwiches. For some reason Effie was staring hard at Jessie.

'What on earth has Jessie gone and done to herself?'

I peered over my glasses. 'She looks all right to me. In fact, she looks rather well.'

Effie's mouth squinched up even further. 'Exactly. She looks better than she has any right to.'

Jessie was breezing along, between the other tables. Her usual tread was listless and heavy. She had worked here eighteen years and she despised her work. She had told us so on many occasions. We had speculated repeatedly on what it was that kept Jessie tethered to a job she hated. Maybe it was a blackmail thing, and the proprietress of the Christmas Hotel *had* something on Jessie. Or maybe Jessie was a timid kind of person who feared leaving a situation she loathed because the thought of the outside world was even more terrible. Who knew? We were too polite to ask her. As it was, we were used to Jessie's quietly corrosive despair. Today, though, she was looking positively jaunty.

'She looks twenty years younger!' Effie cried.

Surely she was exaggerating, I thought. But it wasn't like Effie to resort to hyperbole. I waited until our waitress and our afternoon tea had arrived and then I could properly stare at Jessie.

And it was true! Where were her deeply-etched wrinkles? Where was her scraggy old chicken neck?

'Ladies!' she grinned. 'How lovely to see you.'

Where was her surliness, her migrainey frown?

'What on Earth has happened to you?' Effie demanded crisply.

Jessie shook out her golden (golden!) perm and treated us to a dazzling (dazzling!) grin. 'Ladies...' she announced. 'I have had a make-over.'

Her complexion was marvellous. She had a kind of glow about her. We basked in it, incredulous, as she wielded her tongs, popping cakes onto plates; sliding tea cups before us.

Effie could restrain herself no more. 'But it's impossible!' she burst out. 'No beauty parlour is *that* good.'

I winced at this. Usually it's me being as tactless as that. Jessie gave a carefree laugh. This in itself was alarming. We had never heard her sound carefree before. She let out a volley of shrill guffaws, that rang out and bounced off the glass of the conservatory. Pensioners at the other tables glanced up from their tea and their sherry and Christmas pudding. Jessie? Chortling? In a carefree fashion?

'It's all right,' she smiled down at Effie and I. 'I don't mind. You can say it. It's impossible that I should look so much better. No one could have made the old, careworn Jessie look like this. What a feat! It's amazing, I know. Last time you saw me I was like an old, wrung-out dishrag. All disappointment and bitterness. I know that better than anyone.'

She gave the teapot an energetic swirl and poured our tea for us. We leaned in closer, to hear her secret. 'Even I don't quite believe this miraculous transformation,' she said, lowering her voice. 'I woke up on Saturday morning and I dashed to my mirror. I did the same on Sunday, and the same this morning. Just to check that it was true. I can't believe my luck. I've dropped twenty five years. As if they never even happened to me. I've dropped the worst twenty five years of my life.'

'But,' gasped Effie. 'How?'

'It happened on Friday,' said Jessie. 'It cost a whole two months' wages. But I went to that new place, up Frances's Passage. You must have seen the adverts in the Gazette?'

'Adverts..?' Effie hadn't seen the local paper. But I had.

'The Deadly Boutique,' Jessie said, giving us that glorious smile again, 'has just opened for business. I was one of the first.'

'Deadly?' sniffed Effie. 'Why's it called Deadly?'

I must say, the adjective had rung alarm bells with me, too, when I clapped eyes on the advertisement.

'I don't know!' cried Jessie. 'Who cares? Look at me! I'm fantastic!'

§

That was as much as we heard about it, for now.

Effie was keen on pumping Jessie for more details, and I wouldn't have minded hearing more about this boutique place, too, but suddenly Jessie turned shifty.

'I'm sorry, ladies. I can't stand here chatting all day.' She gulped. 'I keep getting into trouble for chatting with guests. Madam doesn't like it.'

'Madam' was how all the staff at the Christmas Hotel referred to the proprietress. To me, there was something old-fashioned and even sinister about this nomenclature. Jessie looked perturbed. 'I can't go upsetting her. I've drawn a lot of attention already, due to my make-over, and Madam isn't very happy at all.'

'Hmm,' mused Effie, looking troubled. Then she smiled at Jessie. 'You run along then, my dear. We'll see you later.'

'Are you coming to the pie and peas supper on Wednesday evening?' Jessie asked. 'Shall I put your names down?'

Effie frowned. 'Is this a new thing?' I could tell she thought it sounded rather common.

'It's bingo as well, isn't it?' I asked Jessie. 'What a delightful combination! Sign us up, Jessie. We'll both be there!'

We received another dazzling smile from Jessie, and then she was off, shoving that hostess trolley along through the thick carpeting with a lot more vigour than it was used to. I watched Effie sigh heavily.

'Pie and peas and bingo,' she tutted. 'Honestly, Brenda.'

'At least we'll get a chance to quiz Jessie further,' I said, tapping my nose.

§

It was from that point onwards that I think you could say that Effie and I were officially *intrigued*.

We both knew - deep down in our waters - that something very strange was going on. No amount of primping and pampering and preening in some beautician's parlour could change a woman so much. We really hadn't been exaggerating when we said that Jessie had shed twenty five years. She'd slung those years like Gypsy Rose Lee would fling off her long satin gloves.

Effie and I ambled along the breezy front, down the hill, walking off our heavy tea, both musing over Jessie's transformation.

'She said it was like being mesmerized,' I shouted, above the crash and boom of the surf.

'Hm?'

'She let that much out,' I said. 'Being done up... being titivated at the Deadly Boutique was like being mesmerized. That was how she put it. She said she was in a lovely trance, the whole time.'

'Yes,' purred Effie. 'I heard her. It was all most interesting, wasn't it?'

I could feel that we were at the beginning of a whole new crazy adventure. We were at the still point before the storm.

One of the things that Effie and I had discovered about each other – very early on in our friendship – was that there was nothing that either of us liked better than a bloody good mystery. They kept our minds active. They kept us limbered up – mentally, so to speak. No matter how trivial or how earth-shattering – we both liked something mysterious and – dare I say it – even spooky to keep us occupied in our spinstery decrepitude.

Right now, treading on the gold and crimson leaf mulch and tasting the stiff salt breeze of the North Sea, we knew we were on the brink of something grand.

§

I returned to my home, my glorious B+B to get on with my work. Effie went marching off to hers next door after issuing a curt goodbye. There's nothing sentimental in Effie. She's not what you would call a clingy friend. That suits me fine. Off she went, in through her ground floor junk shop, and up into her echoing rooms upstairs.

It must be gloomy for her. Lonely, up there.

I think she prizes her solitude, as do I.

That Monday I had no paying guests. The season had wound down to a standstill and I had only a few bookings lined up in the next couple of months. That was no reason, however, to let things slide. I anticipated a headily enjoyable evening scrubbing out the four bathrooms. Getting the old baking soda going. Sloshing around the place with the mop.

And maybe I'd have a lovely deep bath and pamper myself a bit.

As you can see, I was thinking about make-overs.

But there was no way I could visit the Deadly Boutique. I wouldn't let any beautician lay their hands on me. No matter how skilled or magical they were. I simply couldn't let them touch me.

I can't let anyone get that close.

In the eyes of the world I have to look like an unobtrusive old woman. I have to draw scant attention.

How old am I?

In the eyes of the world, and the eyes of this town, I am coming up to pension age. Effie keeps asking when I'll be due for my bus pass. She's guessed it must be soon. She already has hers and she isn't too proud to get on the buses for nothing. Effie says that when I get mine, we'll go on trips together, up the wild north coast, and count the pennies we'll be saving. I haven't the heart to tell her my pension will never come. I can't bring myself to say that I'm not on the official records. Really, I don't exist. It's hard to explain that to your best friend.

Effie thinks I'm a marvel – she's told me so – for the way I've kept my youth and vitality. I know she means this must be a compensation for being so plain. 'Rather plain,' is the worst thing I have heard Effie say about a woman. She has no compunction about passing comment on people's looks in public, even within their hearing. Effie has the blithe air of someone who was beautiful in her youth. She can't understand how others may be upset by having their appearances remarked upon. She is a subtle thinker, Effie – but she doesn't understand *feelings*.

And yet, she has never asked about the scars on my face. Perhaps she is too polite to ask. Not being the type to stare into mirrors much, I forget that they are there. For whole days at a time I can forget how I look. I enjoy running my fingers along the puckers and gathers of my scars. But I try not to do it in company, because people seem to find it disconcerting.

I have always used a lot of make-up. There is something satisfying about plying on layers of paint and grease, knowing that you are still the same person underneath, even in disguise. I have always found it steadying to know myself exactly.

These were the lines my thoughts were running on, that Monday evening, as I set upon my chores. My hands were rough and crabbed with scrubbing and my knees ached with kneeling on lino. I had my bath in my claw-footed tub, up in my attic and I relaxed at last, and found myself dwelling on these very selfish and self-absorbed thoughts.

It was Jessie who had put me in this frame of mind. Regressing herself and making herself over. She had become a better woman.

That's what I've spent my long, long life doing. Learning to be a better woman.

After I hoisted myself out of my bath and, when I was all cosy in dressing gown and slippers, with some oily black jazz LP going round and round, crackling away, I allowed myself a little weep.

It's not often I indulge myself like this, believe me. Sometimes it all catches up with you.

My life's been quite harrowing. I'm so grateful that, these past months, I find myself landed in this safe new harbour.

Sometimes I still have a little cry.

I am alone on this earth. No siblings nor children to divert or confuse me. I have only ever been perfectly myself, alone. And that perfect self takes the eyelashes and sticks them on with glue; each black lash long as a spider's leg. And she washes, combs and fluffs up her various wigs. I have always wanted to blend in, to be one more barely-visible woman.

I always imagined I could draw nearer to the world of human beings and believe myself part of them.

Here I am in Whitby. The homely, caring Bed and Breakfast lady with the air of quiet authority. When I first came here I listened to the screaming, wheeling gulls. From the jetty I watched the shot grey silk of the perplexing sea. I could smell the vinegary warmth of the fish and chips the holiday people on the prom were eating. I might have thrown in the towel right then.

What am I? A freak of supernature. A thing of shreds and patches. I might have killed myself long ago. But I haven't.

§

As you may have guessed already, I'm extremely proud of my B+B. It cost me an arm and a leg. I'd been saving for years and years. I began with nothing: a few silver coins, which I deposited – several lifetimes ago, it seems like. And I went wandering, looking for a place to settle. By the time I found this house, my savings had grown. I had sufficient.

I have three guest rooms, and my own small set of rooms in the attic. This house, and Effie's ancient family pile next door, are set upon one of the most sloping, perilous streets in our town. Effie is further down the hill and has a ground floor entrance. My downstairs is a small grocers belonging to an Indian family. Quite handy.

I like being slightly higher up. I love living in the eaves of the building. The old mad woman in her spruce and tidy attic. I have a tiny garden where I grow geraniums and I can poke my head out of the skylight and get a glimpse of the turbulent sea and the rocks and the abbey.

This is my little queendom. Whole days can pass, when I don't see anyone at all, and that doesn't bother me one jot. I'm quite happy entertaining myself and doing all the chores I set myself.

That Tuesday was one of those distracted, solitary days. I polished and baked and hummed little tunes to myself. And then, in the early afternoon, the phone went. Guests!

It was a very polite young woman, who said she was a researcher on a cable TV show.

'A TV show?' I frowned.

'Yes, I wrote to you, remember? I asked about booking three rooms for our crew at the end of the month.'

Of course. Now I remembered. The TV people at the end of the month. I hadn't replied to her letter. I'd let it slide by. I didn't want showbiz people poking around in my place. Filming things and asking questions.

'You see, everywhere seems to be booked up that weekend,' the researcher girl was going on. 'It's one of the big pagan festivals or something, and all the B+B's and hotels in your town are chockablock...'

'Well,' I said. 'They would be.'

'So, we thought we'd check back with you, to see if your place was available.'

I twiddled the phone cord round. 'Oh, go on then. I suppose I can fit you in. Three rooms, you say?' Business was business, I reckoned. I needed to make a living.

'Three rooms,' she said. 'There's the presenter, Eunice. And a girl who does hair and make-up. And there's Brian, the psychic.'

'The what?'

'The psychic. You know the show, don't you?'

'I'm afraid I don't.'

'We're on Cable. It's the one where they spend the night in a haunted house and film themselves in infra red getting more and more scared, and trying to call up the spirits of the dead.'

'What?' I could feel my heart thudding alarmingly inside my chest. 'You're not planning on doing... a whole lot of unsavoury practices round my house, are you?'

The researcher chuckled. 'To be honest, I think it's a lot of nonsense. I think Brian fakes it, half the time when he cracks on he's possessed. But it's a popular show. There's a hunger for this kind of spooky stuff.'

'I know,' I nodded. 'But you didn't answer. I asked if you were investigating me... my house.'

'Oh no,' she laughed. 'Next door. Some old junk shop next door that an old dear owns. She was the one who called us in.'

'Effie!' I burst out. 'She called you in?'

'Oh, yes,' said the girl. 'She was very keen. Quite a fan of Brian the psychic, she is. And she reckons there are some queer old spirits round her place.'

'I see,' I said. I wondered why she never told me about this, as I took down further details and particulars in my green leather guest book. I made the researcher girl spell out every name, including the name of the TV show itself. '*Manifest Yourself!*' it was apparently called. 'With an exclamation mark,' the girl prompted. 'The exclamation mark is important. It puts across that wonderful sense of urgency Brian and the team can conjure up.'

'Hm,' I said. 'I must say, I don't hold with dabbling with this kind of thing. I've seen some very nasty things happen along those lines.'

The girl shrugged this off. 'Like I say, this is all faked. It's only showbiz!'

And then she was gone, having booked the team in for the end of the month. It was still a couple of weeks away. Maybe it was nothing to fret about anyway.

I flung on a housecoat and hurried downstairs to the alleyway. I was going to beard Effie in her den. What was she up to? Inviting TV shows and not telling me?

It was dusk. A fine, clinging mist was snaking up the cobbled alley and, when I turned into the sloping main street, I saw that it was inching its way in thick scarves and smothering all in its path. I gave an involuntary shiver as I turned to Effie's front door and rapped on the thick glass.

The shop inside was dark. Was it past closing time? I'd lost all sense of time. I peered inside at the battered copper kettles and cracked ceramics and mottled books in tottering stacks. Filthy old place. I wished she'd get shot of the whole lot. It should have been a house make-over show she'd invited. Not ghost hunters.

As I thought that phrase – 'make-over' – to myself, another shudder went through me, just as if someone had walked on my grave.

Effie was out, that much was certain. I'd given her bell a good old ring. There was no way she'd not hear that. She was out somewhere for definite. Out in the descending fog and the indigo twilight. I don't know why... but that made me a little nervous on her account.

§

And I was right!

I should trust my instincts better, after all these years. When my hackles go up, and all the hairs on my back stand on end, that's a sure sign that something horrible is going on, somewhere close.

Poor Effie was having a terrible time, just a few streets away. In a premises hidden away up an alley called Frances' Passage.

Effie had snuck out to visit The Deadly Boutique. She had gone out investigating alone.

It was only much later that evening that I got to hear about it.

§

I was dozing in front of my little fire that night, when there came all this hullaballoo from the alleyway. Someone was banging away at my front door, just about breaking it down. I came awake with an almighty jolt. I staggered, all befuddled, down the stairs. My dreams had been as lurid and odd as ever and I hadn't had a chance to wake properly.

I flung open the door onto darkness, and Effie standing there, pale with shock and her eyes all red.

'I'm a vain, stupid woman,' she wailed, before bursting into tears. 'I've only just escaped with my life, Brenda!' Then she fell into my arms. She was only the weight of a sackful of leaves.

Questions could wait. I hoisted her easily in my arms and hefted her up to the attic, where soon she was installed in front of the fire. After some moments I had it blazing again, and putting some colour back into those cheeks of hers. Effie slugged back the brandy

I gave her and asked for another. I'd never seen her drink so much, and I'd never seen her cry before.

Again a shudder went through me. Foreboding. A not wholly unpleasant tingle of foreboding went through me.

At last Effie glanced across at me and fixed her pale, watery eyes on mine. 'We must put a stop to them, Brenda,' she said. 'They're up to no good whatsoever.'

I already knew who she was talking about.

'You daft old mare,' I cursed her. 'You went there, didn't you? By yourself? That's why you called yourself vain just now. You went to the Deadly Boutique tonight. For a secret make-over!'

Effie stirred uncomfortably in her armchair. I'd given her the most comfortable seat in the house. I wasn't sure that she deserved it. Sneaking about by herself like that. Investigating things on her own. I thought it was understood by now: we would only investigate these matters together. We needed each other to depend on. We needed back-up.

But then... This investigation wasn't the only thing Effie had planned alone lately. I was reminded, suddenly, of 'Manifest Yourself!' and how she had arranged to hold a televised séance and ghost hunt in her house – all without informing me..!

What kind of friend was Effie turning out to be?

I could feel my old, battered heart steeling itself against her. But then I looked at her pouchy, tear-smudged face and I relented. Poor old dear. I think she'd realised she'd bitten off more than she could chew. Next time she'd make sure Brenda was with her. No fear.

'What happened?' I asked.

Effie gulped. 'Oh, Brenda. It was awful.' For a moment I thought she was going to cry again, but she swallowed it down. I noticed that she was wearing her best woollen suit and had pinned her favourite brooch to the lapel. This added to the pathos somehow: as if she had wanted to look her best, even as she arrived at The Deadly Boutique.

I urged her, 'What did they *do* to you, Effie?'

'I didn't give them the chance to do much at all,' she said. 'As you can see, they didn't have time to make me over, and do whatever terrible thing it is they'd planned on doing. I haven't suddenly shed twenty years, like poor old Jessie. Thank goodness.'

'Start at the beginning,' I told her.

Effie swallowed the rest of her second lot of medicinal brandy and considered. 'I didn't mean to go there. I hadn't made an appointment or anything. I just took a little wander down the Prom this afternoon, before the sea mist came in and I thought... Well, it wouldn't hurt to have a look at the outside of this place. To check in case there was anything suspicious about it. You have to admit, Brenda. We were both pretty intrigued, yesterday afternoon, what with Jessie and all. If you'd been out today, you'd have done the same as me...'

I harrumphed. 'I wouldn't have got myself into trouble. I'd have had more sense than that, I hope.'

'There was no escaping it!' Effie gasped. 'Really! The things they're up to! It's wicked. They won't rest until... until... every woman in town has had a make-over... and been put into The Deadly Machine.'

Effie was jumping ahead of herself again. I glugged us out another shot of the old brandy and found that the drink soon straightened out the narrative.

Effie told me how she had ventured up the shady, cobbled alleyway - almost unwillingly - as if she was acting under some weird influence. That put me in mind of what Jessie had said: that she had felt herself being mesmerized by the owner of the Boutique. And so, drawn away from the straight and narrow of her late afternoon constitutional, Effie had strayed into Frances's Passage. On the way, she passed a young woman in a plastic mac and a rain hood. She was pulling the hood down over her eyes, and the collar up around her ears. She was scooting past Effie as if she didn't want to be observed quitting The Deadly Boutique.

And here was that establishment itself. The black and gold enamel paint of its elaborate sign still looked wet and fresh. The front windows displayed nothing but an extravagant spray of tropical flowers. Effie peered through the distorting glass, and found herself staring at a livid green caterpillar – a disgusting thing – inching its horrid way inside the dewy whorl of a lily. It was munch-munch-munching through the fleshy hood.

'I've never seen such unnatural-looking blooms,' Effie told me.

It was while she was thus bent over, peeping in the front bay like this, that the hissing, insinuating voice came over her shoulder.

'If madam would like to step this way?'

Effie is susceptible to nothing if not flattery.

That quiet voice went on to say: 'It is quite obvious that madam takes a great deal of care with her appearance. Her grooming is immaculate. She looks splendid. However, there is always something that a humble artist, such as myself, can suggest. If madam would like to step into my Boutique...'

Listening to all of this, I was wondering if Effie wasn't building up her part somewhat. Immaculate grooming, indeed. Not that it wasn't true. But trust Effie to feed herself these odd little compliments while she was still supposed to be traumatised.

She turned to see a dapper, quizzical little man stand-ing in the alleyway, blocking her exit. He had thinning, sandy hair, gold-rimmed glasses and a weak chin. His lips, she said, looked very wet. He wore a trimly-cut suit and had a tailor's tape measure hanging round his neck. He looked completely harmless.

'I am Mr Danby,' he smiled. He bowed and this made Effie feel bizarrely powerful. She felt as if she towered above him. 'Welcome to my Deadly Boutique.'

'Why 'Deadly'?' Effie found herself asking, as she allowed herself to be urged into the dim interior.

'Oh,' Mr Danby chuckled. 'A silly whim of mine. It simply describes the effect of the new look we will give you. You will - as the saying has it - 'knock them dead.''

Effie was glancing around at her new surroundings. It was certainly elegant and plush, with more of those strange flowers. The sofas were leopardskin and the walls and floors were carpeted with some kind of shaggy black fur. It felt thrillingly decadent to Effie. There was, as far as she could tell, none of the usual paraphernalia associated with a beautician's: no mirrors and sinks and hair driers and cupboards crammed with powders, paints and unguents.

'I'm not sure,' she said now to Mr Danby. 'I'm not at all sure why I came here. I was intrigued, you see. We met a friend of ours - Jessie - and she's been a visitor here, at The Deadly Boutique. Your – ehm – treatments, whatever they are, seem to have done her a power of good...'

'Ah.' Mr Danby was flipping through a book of handwritten notes kept on the glass-topped counter. 'Oh, yes. Mrs Sturgeon. I remember. She was one of our very first clients. We did a rather good job on her. I recall being particularly proud of Mrs Jessica Sturgeon.' He gave an oily laugh then – whether at his own cleverness, or at poor Jessie's unfortunate surname, Effie couldn't be sure. 'I am pleased that Jessie is spreading the word,' he added. 'I shall have to arrange a reduction in price for her, when she returns tomorrow for her next treatment.'

Effie was surprised. 'She isn't finished?'

'Not quite. She needs a few more sessions. In order to ensure that the work we have begun on her... achieves perfection.' He clasped his tiny, pink hands together and smiled at Effie. 'Now,' he said. 'I think we should stop talking about other people, Ms Jacobs. I think we should concentrate on *you* instead. You have seen what we are capable of here. Just imagine what we could make of you...'

Effie paused here. She was trembling. 'Did you notice?' she whispered to me. 'He knew my name. He seemed to know all about me. He knew what I hate about my... body, and he also knew what I take a secret, foolish pride in. He was a horrid, insinuating little toad. And yet, as he spoke to me – in these very personal, intimate terms – about my nose and my neck and my complexion and neat little ears and my legs and my... my bust ... I felt myself being lulled and drifting off... into a trance... I was being hypnotized, Brenda! Right there and then in The Deadly Boutique! That slimy little devil was putting me under!'

§

There were gaps in Effie's recollection of her bizarre experience at The Deadly Boutique. As she told me the tale she twisted up her face and pulled at her wispy hair with the effort of trying to remember it all. Try as she might, she couldn't fully penetrate the fog in which Mr Danby had ensnared her.

'It went wrong with me,' she said. 'Somehow, the hypnotism didn't fully work. I came to, too soon. I woke up and I was standing inside the machine! It was like a sort of tanning booth, you know the type of thing. But it was different. It wasn't just lit up inside... it was all pulsating weirdly, with flashing lights and clouds and... Oh, Brenda. It was like a nightmare. I was standing there swaying and it was like being on drugs or something. I screamed and screamed, right there inside The Deadly Machine, but nobody came.

Nobody would set me free. I felt like I was going to die.'

'But what is it, Effie? What did it do?'

'I don't know! I could feel... horrid things. Tiny little hands, all over my body. Patting and stroking and primping me. They were kneading me and rolling me about like a lump of dough. I screamed and thrashed about, but to no avail. I was being spun round and round... and I remember thinking: this is it! I'm being... made over!'

I stared at her. She looked exactly the same as she always did. 'What happened? Why didn't the process work?'

'I wasn't docile and still enough, I suppose,' she said, thoughtfully. 'That's why he mesmerizes his victims. So they don't kick about and pummel at the doors in fright at the terrible things that go on inside that machine... Honestly, Brenda. It was like being inside the mind of a maniac!'

'You kicked your way out?' I gasped.

'I never even knew I had that kind of strength!' She looked rather proud at this. 'But that's precisely what I did. I was thrashing about so much, my foot managed to connect with the heavy cubicle door and the thing flew open! And there I was - standing starkers - toppling out into the middle of this white, tiled, laboratory-type place.'

'Starkers!' I cried. 'He undressed you!'

'I suppose he must have,' she said. 'But there wasn't time to be embarrassed.'

I was amazed at Effie. Usually she was so prim. But here she was relating her terrible, nude adventure and barely even raising a blush.

'Mr Danby wasn't there in the laboratory at the back of the Boutique. That devil hadn't even stuck around to see how his handiwork turned out. But his helpers were there. His assistants with the beautifying process. They were milling around me, flapping their arms and shrieking at me. I don't suppose they'd ever known anyone to burst and stagger prematurely out of the make-over machine before. They squealed and shouted, motioning me to get back into that dizzying death-trap. But I wasn't about to take any of their nonsense. I demanded my clothes! I demanded to be set free!'

'But what did they say? Did they explain themselves?'

Effie frowned, concentrating. 'My impressions are pretty scrambled, but I don't think his assistants were even speaking English. They were tiny, like children, in white plastic space suit things. They were squabbling and gibbering in some sort of foreign language. Nasty-sounding.' Her eyes widened as she pictured them. 'They were like little children, but they had awful, withered up, ancient faces, like little primates.'

I tried to picture Effie, surrounded by these panicked, nasty beings, bellowing for her clothes back.

'I grabbed hold of one and twisted its arm, very hard and spitefully. Remember that jujitsu class I took for a while in the summer? Came in handy. I was so riled, I could have broken the creature's arms. I must have looked a fearsome sight, because they brought my clothes, all neatly folded, and stood back as I quickly dressed. Then they showed me to the back door and pushed me out into the night, as peremptorily as their master had urged me through the front entrance. They knew the process had gone wrong, evidently, and they wanted me off the premises immediately. I staggered out into the misty night, finding myself in a very ordinary back yard in Frances's Passage. It took me a matter of minutes to wander the labyrinth of alleys and to find myself back at the Prom. I came straight here.' She held out her glass for brandy. 'Brenda, can I stay here, tonight? I keep thinking about that insinuating little man and his monkey-like women assistants. I fear that they'll come after me in the night.'

'Of course!' I cried. 'I've three rooms, all clean and made up...'

Effie nodded, cradling her balloon glass with both hands. 'It was one of the most hair-raising experiences of my life.'

'What would have happened,' I said slowly, 'if the hypnotism had worked properly? If you'd stayed in the machine till the end of the process?'

'I suppose I'd be the same as Jessie. A full twenty five years younger.'

I nodded. 'You must be more strong-willed than Jessie. To withstand the mesmerizing.'

She agreed. 'I've always known my own mind, that's true.'

'But what would be so wrong about regressing twenty five years? Surely the process was only horrible because you woke up too early...'

Effie's eyes looked haunted. She looked ghastly and drawn. 'I can't explain it fully, Brenda. But it was evil, whatever it was. There is something in that machine, and in that Boutique... and it isn't right. Whatever they are doing, it isn't for the good of their clients. The purpose of the Deadly Machine isn't just giving women make-overs. There's more to it than that. I could feel it.'

Just then Effie declared herself exhausted. I swept into action. I was the dedicated and professional B+B lady: showing my guest to her room downstairs. Making sure she had everything; making sure of her comfort.

'Tomorrow,' I promised her. 'Tomorrow we can start to get to the bottom of this business.'

She lay back in the clean, crisp linen of my best guest room. 'When I close my eyes... I can still see the swirling mist and lights inside that machine. It felt terrible, Brenda. I could feel it pulling and sucking at me... sucking the time and the years and all my experience away from me...'

§

I let Effie sleep in for much of the next morning. I knew it wasn't like her to sleep so late. Usually you can hear her rattling about in that huge house of hers next door, and she seems to rise even before I do. She doesn't half clatter around amongst all that dusty junk. It's rather odd, really: she sounds so careless and rackety within the privacy of her own four walls. And yet, when you see her and out about she's so proper and tidy.

On the Wednesday morning, however, she was sleeping placidly in my B+B, recovering from the shock of her make-over ordeal. At eleven I took in a tray with a modestly tempting breakfast of kippers. She seemed muddled but grateful. I left her to it and, struck by a certain impulse, rang the Christmas Hotel.

'I'd like to be put through to the staff quarters,' I told the girl on the reception desk.

'Madam doesn't like the phone lines to be used by the staff,' I was told, quite frostily.

'I don't care about that,' I said. 'Madam will just have to lump it. This is an emergency.' I could hear the grumbling in the background as I was put through to the relevant line. There was a snatch of a Christmassy jingle, and then the phone rang for a good few minutes. Then there came a male voice. Young-sounding.

'I'm afraid you've missed Jessie,' he told me. 'She went out first thing. I'm her nephew, Robert. Can I pass a message on for you?'

'Oh,' I said, surprised. 'Robert! She's told me all about you. She said how she'd got you a job for the autumn season. Have you just started? How are you liking it?'

He sounded sardonic in his reply. 'I'm not wholly convinced I'll make a career as a Christmas elf. But it's ok, I suppose. For a while. And it's nice to spend time with my Aunt Jessie. We've always got on well.'

'I'm Brenda. I'm an acquaintance... Well, a friend, really, of your Aunt's.'

'Good,' he said. 'She could do with some sensible people on the outside, unconnected with this madhouse. She could do with some people to talk some sense into her.'

'Sense?' I said. 'What about?'

Robert the elf sighed heavily. 'This make-over business. I think she's taking it too far. It's like an obsession with her. I mean, fair enough, they've done an amazing job on her so far. She looks much, much better than she has done for years. But it's all she'll talk about! She's swanning around this hotel like a pin-up girl for The Deadly Boutique.'

'I know,' I said. 'We saw her. We were amazed by her. It's certainly impressive. It's almost uncanny.'

Robert snorted. 'Uncanny is exactly what I'd call it.' He sighed. 'Now she's got all the old dears in this place stirred up about it. All the old witches here have been trooping down to that Boutique place. They can't wait to get done! They're all scraping their pennies together and making appointments.'

My heart rate stepped up at this. I imagined queues of old women, anxious to be put through the same weird trauma as Effie.

'You know, Robert... I think they should be warned. I don't think anyone is doing themselves any favours by visiting this Deadly Boutique.'

'I think you're right, Brenda,' he said. 'I've tried to tell my aunt that. I tried this morning, first thing. But she won't listen. All she can think about is the good it's doing her. How now, at the age of sixty six, she looks forty one and how, after her next appointment, she'll end up looking even younger. In her twenties, perhaps. Well, that's not natural, is it? There must be some hidden catch.'

I liked this Robert. He seemed a very sensible young man to me. 'Exactly my thinking. We need to stop Jessie from returning there.'

'But...' he said. 'It's her morning off. She's already there! She's at The Deadly Boutique right now!'

§

For the size I am, I'm quite nimble on my pins. Even though the rest of me can seem a bit ungainly I can cut a dash when I want to. I can move quickly and stealthily and that's precisely what I did, having finished on the phone with Jessie's helpful nephew. I didn't tell Effie I was nipping out. She'd only want to accompany me and, despite her protestations, I could tell she was still shaken up by her recent escapades.

It was too early for her to return to the Boutique.

So I went by myself.

I ran down our hill and through the narrow streets towards the Promenade. I ignored neighbours and acquaintances alike as I barrelled along, filled with ire and determination. When I came to Frances's Passage I took a deep breath and stepped bravely into its chilly confines. There was a waft of something clammy and evil down this ginnel. It was obvious to me, straight away: there was evil here. I surveyed the frontage of the Boutique, and everything was as Effie had described it, down to the outrageous flowers flaunting themselves in the bow window.

The door was locked. A sign was hanging on the inside, claiming that the place was closed. I knew that couldn't be right. I knew that Jessie Sturgeon was inside there, probably crammed inside the Deadly Machine, having goodness knows what done to her. I rapped heavily upon the shiny black door. I pushed hard against the wood with my shoulder.

Nothing. And, when I pressed my ear to the glass panels, I couldn't hear a thing. Not a dicky-bird.

It wasn't the kind of silence that makes you think the interior is deserted: that everyone has packed up and taken a day off. It was the kind of silence that makes you think of creeping, underhand, untrustworthy things. Of foul deeds going on, just out of view. Of nefarious people hiding their wicked selves away until you grow bored and decide to leave them to it...

I decided I'd sneak around the back. Effie had said they'd let her out the back door, into what appeared to be an ordinary yard. There was an elaborate network of back alleys and interconnecting yards, as there was in all of these Victorian warrens, but I was sure to find the correct one in the end. It would just take perseverance.

I shivered at the church clock, bonging out the hour. Eleven o'clock. Jessie's appointment had been for ten, her nephew had told me. I was already too late.

All of those backyards looked the same. Concrete and cobbles, lichen and moss. Dripping grates and drainpipes and cold, grey stone. I went creeping about, clattering past bins and hauling myself up to peep over crumbling walls. It's a wonder I wasn't mistaken for a burglar. But it was uncanny. There was no one about. No net curtains twitching, no one bringing out the rubbish. Not even an old moggy prowling about the place. Silence. No one.

Except... one particular building. Anonymous as the rest. But the back door was silvery. It was a new, solid-looking metal door. As I watched, perched halfway up a wall, that door came open and out came three of the strangest-looking women I have ever seen. They were carrying with them large glass bottles filled with a variety of greenish-coloured liquids. They had a selection of hoses and funnels and they were quietly gabbling away to each other in a strange tongue.

I shrank away, so they wouldn't see me. I narrowed my eyes, appalled at the sight of them. All I can say is that Effie was actually quite generous when she described these assistants to Mr Danby as withered-up primate women. They were, to my eyes, the most peculiarly horrid creatures I have ever seen. Their flesh had turned white like fish-bellies and their hair was colourless and stringy. They were the height of infants and they wore bizarrely unflattering boiler suits. They gibbered and whispered and, I realised, they were pouring the bright green liquids down the drains. It ran, glistening and oily, into the sewers and the little women gathered to watch it go.

I couldn't guess what it was they were up to. It looked to me as if they were disposing of some horrid byproduct of their nasty experiments.

Then, just as soon as they had appeared, the weird assistants had hurried back indoors and the silver door was slammed shut once again.

There had been no sign of Jessie. For all my scrambling about and barking my shins and knees, I had learned nothing whatsoever.

I hadn't liked the look of that green fluid, though. It was like bitterness and bile, and they were siphoning it straight into the water system...

§

Effie is the type to go pottering around auction houses and stately homes. Her idea of an evening's entertainment is to attend a concert, some soothing and hummable classical thing. It certainly isn't her idea of fun to go to a pie and peas supper, and to suffer the tawdry thrills of a game of bingo.

But that night we both had to attend The Christmas Hotel. Effie muttered only a few complaints as we trip-trapped up the sloping streets to the smart row at the top of our town.

The view out to sea was dramatic that night. The clouds were all plumped up and tempestuous. The sea birds were weirdly quiet.

On the way up there I filled Effie in on my adventure in the back alley.

'Green liquids,' she frowned.

'Do you think they're trying to poison everyone in the town?' I asked her. 'Pouring something nasty into the water system...'

'It doesn't sound like it to me,' she said. 'It sounds more like they're disposing of something they don't need. There'd be easier ways of poisoning everyone than chucking things in the sewers. Poisoned pies and peas, for example.'

'I do hope Jessie is all right,' I sighed.

'We'll soon find out, won't we?' said Effie heartily. She was displaying a good deal more bravado than I expected her to. As she led the way through the hotel's grand entrance, I reflected that Effie's dander was up now. She had been scared, mortally scared, the previous evening, and now she would be absolutely determined to sort this business out. She had an enemy in her sights: Mr Danby. He had done something nasty and strange to her, and this made the business quite straightforward in Effie's mind. She would have to sort him out.

Meanwhile... it was Christmas time all over again in The Christmas Hotel.

Everything that could be, had been well and truly trimmed with tinsel, holly, mistletoe and fake snow. Carols rang out through hidden speakers: about three or four different ones, all at once, in a weird, festive cacophony. Party hooters and crackers were going off and we were offered, as always, a cupful of mulled wine from the silver tureen at the reception desk, as soon as we stepped inside.

Effie and I took some, relishing the spiced warmth of the wine. We'd need to be fortified indeed, if this macabre adventure carried on as it had begun. Behind the receptionist's desk and wielding the ladle was a tall, rather good-looking young man who nodded knowingly at us.

'It's me,' he said. 'Robert. You *are* Brenda, aren't you?'

His friendliness and his searching glance into my face made me feel very self-conscious. I wasn't used to that degree of scrutiny.

'Yes,' I mumbled. 'You're Jessie's nephew?'

He was, of course, dressed in one of the hotel's quite absurd elf outfits. The indignity of it! These skinny, lanky boys were forced to wear skin-tight green felt one-piece suits with green pointy hats and stick-on pointy ears. The poor thing looked quite habituated to his costume, even the two dots of red on his cheeks and the fake freckles across his nose. I introduced him quickly to Effie.

'I knew it was you two, soon as you walked in. Aunty Jessie said you were both unmistakable.'

Now I felt even more self-conscious. I felt like a great lumbering, hideous creature. My scarred, twisted flesh itched and blushed under the layers of make-up. I struggled to listen as the boy went on talking. He talked so insouciantly: he was so handsome and young, I found myself staring, in a trance of my own self-loathing.

'So Jessie is here?' barked Effie, suddenly, breaking me out of my spell. 'She returned safely from her appointment at the boutique this morning?'

'Oh yes,' he said. 'She came back at lunch time, ready for her afternoon shift. I saw her briefly and she seemed fine. She was relaxed and happy and... well, the treatment hadn't had such a dramatic effect this time. She'd only regressed a further couple of years. Nothing as drastic as last time. I must say, she seemed disappointed by that.'

'She should think herself lucky that she's still alive,' Effie said bitterly.

Robert looked shocked.

'Effie's been there,' I explained. 'She knows just what...'

We were interrupted quite rudely then, by a huge, raucous, hectoring voice that cut through our conversation from the direction of the old fashioned lift cage. We three turned quickly and guiltily to see who was calling.

Of course we already knew who it was.

There, in her motorized scooter, Christmas green and red, bedecked with tinsel and bows and mistletoe, sat the gargantuan form of Madam: the owner, manageress and genius of The Christmas Hotel. We didn't know her real name. We knew her only as Mrs Claus and, seeing her there, all thirty stone of her clad in red velvet with a wreath of holly leaves crowning her snowy bouffant, there was no other name that would have suited her. She advanced on us in her juddering scooter, flanked by a royal guard of Elves, all uniformed as Robert; all of them solemn with yuletide responsibilities.

'Welcome! Welcome!' she bellowed at us. 'It's so rare to see you two at one of my evening gatherings!'

Her face was bright red. At first it looked like makeup: like the high red spots on the elves' cheeks. But her face was crazed with broken veins. The reek of spirits came wafting off her, very powerfully.

'Robert!' she yelled. 'I need you to call the bingo numbers. You've got the clearest and nicest speaking voice of all my elves.'

Astonished, we watched Robert scurry around the desk and away into the main dining room to do her bidding. All of the elves were over-anxious to please her. Effie and I exchanged a glance at this.

'Ladies,' Mrs Claus simpered. 'We must hurry and take our places. Otherwise we will be left with no dinner. That lot through there can be like gannets.'

She went trundling off, elves marching along beside her.

'They're all scared of her,' Effie said.

'They certainly seem to be,' I frowned. 'Even Robert, and he seems so sensible.'

'I wonder what's going on.' Effie shuddered. 'I hate this creepy place. It used to be so lovely and classy when I was a little girl. My father used to bring me for tea on my birthdays. She's spoiled it. She's made it gaudy and sickly sweet...'

I followed Effie into the dining hall, where the walls rang with false jollity and edgy jubilation. A heavy scent of gravy hung in the air as the waitresses went round with their trollies. Effie was right. Underneath the gilt and the crepe paper, there was something rotten and wrong about The Christmas Hotel. But perhaps that was another mystery. One for another day, maybe.

§

I actually enjoy a good game of bingo. I was well aware of Effie's withering scorn as I brought my dabbing-pen down on my numbers. I was within a whisker of winning one of the later games and, I must admit it, I got quite carried away by it all, wailing out in disappointment when someone called 'House!' just ahead of me.

'Well,' sniffed Effie. 'I'm glad that's at an end.'

She had done nothing but complain all evening. Her peas had been cold, her pie too hot, so that she had burned her mouth. The game had been too simplistic for her, and then it had gone too fast, so that – what with her arthritis – she couldn't hope to keep up.

'Didn't Robert do a good job with calling out the numbers?' I nodded over at the tall boy, still standing behind the glass tank of coloured balls.

'Is he a nancy boy?' Effie asked loudly. 'I've nothing against them, mind you. He seems to be that way, doesn't he?'

I found myself blushing again, and hushed her. 'Don't be so rude.'

'There's nothing rude in it,' Effie protested. 'It's just a statement of fact. I'm sure he wouldn't be offended.'

'Oh, I'm sure.' I said. 'Nancy boy, indeed. What an awful thing to call the lad.'

Effie pursed her lips, glaring at me narrowly. 'Not all of us are ashamed of what we are, Brenda,' she said, in a much lower voice. 'Not all of us keep a tin lid on who and what we are.'

I turned away from her abruptly. She was being very peculiar. I didn't know what she meant at all. Was she still talking about Robert? Or was she trying to tell me something about herself? Or... No. She was having a dig at me, wasn't she? She was talking about my own secretiveness. She was referring to the way I don't ever talk about myself. Where I'm from. Who my people are. Who I really am.

Oh, Effie. I can't really tell you. You wouldn't like it. You'd never believe it. You'd think I was crazy. You'd think you were best friends with a crazy woman.

I saw then that it was Jessie coming over to us with her hostess trolley. It was time for coffee and she had sought us out herself, bringing the silver pot and the china cups.

She had come to show herself off to us. Slinkier and younger than ever.

We gasped. She did a twirl and the two of us sat there, agog. We weren't faking it. We didn't have to pretend, or to flatter her. Our mouths hung open in shock and awe, and Jessie laughed at us. She tossed back her head and laughed joyously.

'But... Robert said that, this time, there was less of a change...' I stammered. 'He said he saw you, when you came back from the Boutique at lunch time. He said you were disappointed, because the change was less marked.'

Jessie shrugged gaily. 'Yes! That's how it was, back at lunch time. But... it's like Mr Danby explained to me. As the treatments advance, sometimes they are slower to take a hold. Well! I had a little nap in my room. I drew my curtains and I lay down on my bed and I fell into a perfect, most relaxing sleep. And, when I woke up, just in time for my shift at work... this is how I found myself.'

I looked at Effie, and she was shaking her head slowly. She was as astonished as I was. She looked disturbed, too, as if she was witnessing something that just couldn't be true.

'Look at me! I'm in my twenties again! I look to be no older than twenty three!'

Jessie started to pour our coffee for us.

'God bless Mr Danby,' she sighed. 'Bless him and his magical contraption. He's been sent as a blessing to all of us. To make all our lives perfect and complete. How much we owe him! He is a boon to us. To all womankind!'

As Jessie dropped the sugar cubes into our cups and poured out the cream, I couldn't help thinking: It's driven her crazy. The shock of it all has sent her insane.

§

'But it can't be *right*, can it?' I said.

We were walking along the Prom again. It was our usual route, down from The Christmas Hotel to home, though we usually followed it at tea time, before night had fallen as drastically as this; before the stars had come to gloat over the pulsing, endless sea.

Effie was steeped in thought. She shook her head to clear it and smiled grimly. 'No,' she said. 'Indeed. It can't be *right*.'

'There just has to be a catch,' I said. 'I don't for a second begrudge Jessie her good fortune. I'm delighted for her, in fact. But what's happened to her simply can't have happened. It isn't possible. There has to be some kind of drawback... or payback...'

'Quite,' said Effie. 'The world doesn't work like that, does it? She can't just divest herself of all those long lived years. She can't just set the clock back. It's like fiddling with the gas meter: you'll get found out. We only get one go on the merry-go-round. And she's kidding herself if she thinks she can keep galloping round.'

'Still,' I said. 'She *did* look marvellous.'

'A miracle, she called it.' Effie sighed. I glanced at her as we trundled along. She was grimacing. Her face was hawklike: white as a sheet in the moonlight.

'She said Mr Danby was an angel,' I added. 'An angel sent to improve us all.'

I saw the fury rise up in Effie's face. 'He's nothing of the sort. That's blasphemy, Brenda. She'll see that in the end. She'll regret all of this, in the end.'

I wish I'd never mentioned the angel thing. That religious talk can get Effie really fired up. As I said earlier: I can do without the religiosity, thank you very much. My father was a man obsessed with the idea of God. With the idea of *being* God, mostly.

'Did you hear all the old women?' I said. 'Cooing over her. She even got a round of applause from some of them. She's a walking advertisement.'

'That's what worries me,' Effie said. 'They'll be flocking.'

Now we were at the bottom of the hill, right on the sea front. This was the quickest way back, and yet it took us through the roughest part of the town centre. Here, the amusement arcades were still open: pouring their gaudy golden light into the bay. The music was cheap and tinny and we could hear the crash and tinkle of silver and copper, clunkily mocking the noise of the sea.

'We should have gone the longer way round,' Effie said tersely, eyeing the young people clustered at the entrance. They were loud and loitering by the pin ball machines and those things with grabby mechanical arms and fluffy toys. Effie shrank from their bois-terousness, but I was thinking, oughtn't they to be loud? When else *could* they be loud, other than when they were young? And where else in our tiny backwater town were the youngsters able to make some noise and kick up some fuss? Good luck to them all, I thought, as Effie and I took tight hold of our handbags and marched firmly and bravely past the glowing entrance to Aladdin's Cave.

I didn't say any of these things to Effie, of course. She thinks I'm much too liberal in my outlook. She says she believes in Victorian values.

I don't. I didn't like those much, first time around.

'It's all right,' I told Effie. 'The kids can't even see us. We're invisible to them, two old dames like us. What would they want with us?'

Effie pursed her lips. She was about to reply – sardon-ically, if I knew anything – when suddenly she stopped dead in her tracks. We were directly opposite the en-trance of the arcade and she was staring intently at it, across the road. 'Look!'

I saw immediately who she was pointing at and, instinctively – with the well-honed instincts of now-seasoned investigators – the two of us drew into the shadows.

Emerging from the shabby razzamatazz of the penny arcades was a dapper, fair-haired little man. He was accompanied by five extremely short, unattractive women. They were a familiar and unprepossessing bunch: all of them still wearing their pristine coveralls. All six in this party were gabbling excitedly in their weird language. Effie and I watched, astounded, as they all linked arms with each other and made off down the road, towards *Cod Almighty*, the chip shop at the end of the Prom.

Effie and I stood there, frozen.

Until the moment – just as Mr Danby and his harem slipped into the chip shop – when he turned and very deliberately waved at us. From all that distance away down the street, he fixed us with a twinkling, ironic grin, and gave us a jaunty wave. And all his simian assistants, giggling, did likewise.

§

For the next couple of days or so I tried to put this whole business of the Deadly Boutique out of my head. As I was going about my daily business though I'd get flashbacks to the smug, simpering faces of that awful Mr Danby and his primate women on Wednesday night. It was plain that they were ne'er-do-wells, and they were flaunting it. Only Effie and I could see the truth of this. But what could we do?

The local Gazette carried an interview with the slimy owner of the Boutique. That idiot of a journalist, Rosy Twist, was fawning all over him.

'Women have a duty to stay young and beautiful,' he was quoted as saying. 'I am their humble servant. I have been sent to help them all.'

But why here? Why this small town?

As the weekend approached I kept my eyes and ears open and I moved about the town, buying groceries and scouting about. I saw a number of changed women, all looking very pleased with themselves. It was quite alarming. All these clear complexions. All these newly fresh faces. I don't want to exaggerate – there weren't hundreds of rejuvenated women – but there were enough for it to be remarkable. For it to be obvious that The Deadly Boutique was doing a roaring trade.

Saturday morning I bumped into Robert in Woolworths. I was helping myself to the pic-n-mix. A small vice of mine. Every Saturday morning I'll fill a large paper bag at the pic-n-mix counter: grabbing up handfuls of chocolate limes and mint supremes and sherbert fizzers and anything else I fancy. My hands are rather large and I end up with a large collection of sweets, usually.

'Hello,' he hissed politely and at first I never recognised him without his elf costume. He was in a rather battered flying jacket trimmed in sheepskin. He looked rather fetching. Turns out he's an aficionado of the pic-n-mix counter, too. Liquorice allsorts are his thing.

'I'm looking for something to take Jessie,' he admitted, as we queued to pay. 'She's in the doldrums today.'

'How come?' I said. 'She should be on cloud nine! She was the belle of the ball at the pie and peas.'

Robert's face darkened. 'She's holed herself up in her room. She reckons...' He looked incredulous. 'She says it's backfiring. She says she's... shrinking. Withering up.'

'What?!'

'It'll be all in her head, though,' he added, looking more hopeful than convinced. 'She's always been paranoid about her looks.'

'She's shrinking?'

'I haven't seen her. She won't let anyone in her room. But it can't be true, can it? It's impossible!'

I shrugged, as the girl at the counter put my sweets on the scale. I'd pick-n-mixed even more than usual. 'But what happened to her at the Boutique was impossible, too.'

'You think she might be right? That it's backfiring?' Robert seemed appalled at the thought.

I nodded solemnly at him, thinking: how nice! To have a nephew who really cares about what happens to you.

We parted at the main doors of Woollies. 'Do you think she'll see visitors?'

He shook his head. 'But I'll ask her. She's very fond of you. And Effie.'

I nodded. 'We're going to get to the bottom of this awful business. We're going to sort this Mr Danby out.'

For a moment Robert looked into my face searchingly. 'Yes,' he said. 'I believe you will.'

I realised that I'd come out that morning without applying my make-up as thickly and as comprehensively as usual. As he gazed into my face in the harsh light of the morning, I flinched. He would be able to see the full extent of the scarring on my neck and my temples, underneath the thinnish layer of foundation. What would he think? Car accident? Botched face lift?

But he was discreet and he never said anything. Just nodded, and turned away, carrying his sweets and his newspapers back up the road.

§

At home, I sat in my favourite bobbly green armchair in the attic and wolfed my pic-n-mix absent-mindedly, stewing it all over.

I took a call about a booking for next week. Guests! A whole family of them, coming up from Norfolk. Sounded rather nice. Quiet. They've got two youngish children, which I'm not too keen on. But, so long as they behave themselves... They arrive on Tuesday.

I let things wash back and forth in my head for a while, munching on sherbert fizzers in my bobbly green armchair, deciding on my next move. Next thing, I was sitting bolt upright. I'd decided what to do.

'This time, *I'm* going there,' I told Effie.

She scowled at me. 'Where? What are you talking about?'

She was sitting in the gloomiest recess of her junk shop: at the cluttered old desk right at the back. It was hard even to get to, through the tottering stacks of rubbish, especially if you're my size. Now Effie was rolling her eyes and seeming less than pleased to clap eyes on me.

'To the boutique,' I hissed, through clenched teeth, although there was only one other customer present to hear me.

Effie sighed. 'I do wish you'd stop bursting in here, Brenda, and telling me what you're going to do. Why do you have to go galumphing about so dramatically all the time?'

Effie can be quite short-tempered and sour-faced when she's working in the junk shop. Really, it's best to avoid her when she's in there. It's like she's a different person, operating under the strain and the weight of all that accumulated bric-a-brac. She never chose this life. She feels she simply inherited it, and yet she's done nothing to alter it. Instead she's grown rather bitter and she's best avoided during opening hours.

But today I knew I just had to tell her.

'I've phoned up. I talked to that awful man, and I've made an appointment for myself.'

Effie looked me up and down. 'For a make-over?' I knew what she was insinuating. That I could really do with one. I blushed at this. She was being rather cruel. That was Effie all over. She would never say it outright, but she could infer it with a simple raised eyebrow.

'That's the pretext and the excuse,' I said. 'But I'm just going to get inside the place. I'm infiltrating it. Tonight.'

Effie was twiddling with a propeller pencil. 'I see. What about me?'

My turn to raise an eyebrow. Not quite as elegantly as Effie, perhaps.

'What part do I play in this little escapade, hm?' She had lowered her voice, so that the only other customer – Reverend Small, poking about in the crockery – couldn't hear.

'I didn't think you'd want to go back there!'

'I don't want to,' she sighed impatiently. 'But we're a team, aren't we?'

This was good to hear. I smiled.

'Oh, don't come over all mawkish, Brenda. Just tell me what time and what the plan is.'

'But they'll know you! They'll know it's you that the machine didn't work on.'

'So?' she said. 'I'll just say I got claustrophobic and went doo-lally. I'll just say I'm accompanying you to hold your hand because you're a bit nervy. They won't suspect a thing.'

'Hmmm,' I mused. Mr Danby sounded like a wily one to me. But Effie was right. We were better off going down to the boutique together.

When I told her what Robert reckoned was happening to Jessie, Effie became even more determined.

'Shrinking?' she gasped. 'Wrinkling up?' She shook her head sadly. 'I can believe it. I knew no good would ever come of this. Jessie's overreached herself.' Effie stood up and straightened her smart woollen jacket. 'I'm going to shut up the shop. We've got to prepare ourselves. We've got work to do.'

§

'I knew it! I told my helpers, just this morning. I told them that this would happen. I knew you would return to our establishment. May I take your coat?'

Effie looked the wheedling little man up and down. Utter disdain. 'No, you may not.' She clutched it tighter and glanced in my direction. 'This time it is my friend who requires... your attentions.'

'Aaaah,' purred Mr Danby. He licked this thin, wet lips and feasted his piggy eyes on me. I stared back at him bravely, all the while taking in the details of the boutique. Everything was as Effie had described: the weird, shaggy walls and the rubber plants. 'And your name is...?'

'Brenda,' I said. 'I don't have a surname.'

Effie looked at me sharply, as if to say, what subterfuge is this? No surname?

But it was quite true. I don't.

'Quite so,' said Mr Danby. 'And will Brenda be requiring a full make-over?'

I snorted with laughter. 'What do you think?' I said, with more bravado than I felt. 'Look at me! You've got your work cut out for you here, Mr Danby.'

'Quite so,' he said again, absently. He was making notes in a tiny book, and tapping his pencil against his teeth. 'You are a magnificent specimen, my dear.'

Effie looked shocked at this: both at his forwardness, and his verdict. I blushed, of course, and thanked him.

'You are a very well-built specimen,' Mr Danby added, catching my eye. I looked away.

'Look here,' Effie butted in. 'Will I be able to sit with my friend when you put her inside of that nightmarish contraption of yours in the back room?'

Mr Danby grimaced at the sound of her voice. 'That 'nightmarish contraption' is nothing of the sort, Ms Jacobs. It is a highly-sophisticated and unique device. There is nothing nightmarish or truly deadly about it whatsoever. Oh yes, I know all about your suspicions and your strange ideas regarding me. But sincerely, all I wish is to bring a little light and life and youthfulness into the lives of you ladies. There is no wicked masterplan. No nefarious schemes.' He chuckled.

I must say, standing there listening to all of this in the plush, luxurious reception of The Deadly Boutique, I was inclined to start believing him. He was very smart in his pin stripe suit and his hair smarmed down just so. He was very convincing.

I was being lulled. I was being drawn in. I was starting to imagine what it would be like to be slimmed and primped and smoothed and ironed. To feel new again...

Effie wasn't having any of it. 'I've had your silver tongue before,' she snapped.

'Indeed,' he said.

'I think you're up to no good. What about Jessie, eh?'

'Jessie is a triumph,' he said flatly. 'Any fool can see that.'

'But her nephew claims that she's shrinking! She's wrinkling up!'

'Nonsense,' said Mr Danby sternly. 'Have you seen her with your own eyes?'

'Well, no. But the nephew has no reason to lie...'

'Jessie Sturgeon is a work of art,' he said. 'And, if she continues her treatments here at my boutique, she will continue to be a work of art for a good many years.'

'It's unnatural,' spat Effie. She was getting very worked up about this. Probably the memory of thrashing about inside The Deadly Machine was coming back to her full force.

'Listen to yourself!' Mr Danby laughed. 'You sound like a superstitious fool. A torch-waving peasant crying, 'Kill the beast! Burn it! Get it away from our town!'

My ears pricked up at this. What? What did he mean?

'I'm not superstitious,' said Effie haughtily. 'And I'm by no means a peasant.'

Mr Danby gave a very gallic shrug. 'No matter. You have already spurned our treatments here and I see no further reason to discourse on these matters. We will, of course, send you our bill for the few moments you stole inside our 'contraption.''

'Your bill...!' spluttered Effie.

Smoothly, the little man took hold of my elbow and led me towards an interior door. 'My assistants will help you to prepare for stepping into the machine, Madam Brenda...'

Madam Brenda! I liked that! It sounded rather impressive. I felt like a grand and imperious brothel-owner.

By now I was feeling quite woozy and complaisant. I let him draw me along, away from Effie's side. I was focussing on the boutique owner's cultivated, melodious voice.

'Wait!' cried Effie. 'You've got to let me come in with her. I'm her friend. I'm here to see that no harm comes to her...'

'My helpers are all she needs,' said Mr Danby.

'No!' Effie cried. 'I must come in with her. Brenda! Tell him!'

My voice came out softer and more dreamy than I'd intended. 'Could she, Mr Danby? Could she just sit and wait? She'll be no bother.'

'No bother?' Mr Danby said. 'No bother, you say?'

And then I was rocking gently on my heels. I was swaying back and forth. My ears were filled with reverberating voices: 'No bother?' yelled Mr Danby. 'Brenda!' howled Effie. 'Tell him!' Everything was chiming and echoing like I was in some ancient Jules Verne-like diving suit and their voices were being piped down to the bottom of the sea. My vision narrowed into two tiny points of light... and then nothing.

I was under.

And ready to be made-over.

§

At first it was like being in one of those sensory-deprivation tanks. I lifted my hands in front of my face and couldn't see a thing. It was silent inside, too, and I felt as if I was floating; bobbing about in amniotic fluid.

I should have known this was a mistake. I should never have come here.

But something had compelled me. Was I really under Mr Danby's influence? Or was I being driven along by my own subconscious desires to be born again; to start again? I mulled all of this over in a shambolic, bemused fashion.

I was naked, that much was certain. I blushed with shame, thinking of it. Of divesting myself of all my many layers of cardies and foundation garments, in full view of Effie and those horrid simian assistants. The little women picked up my clothes, piece by piece as I dropped them on the pristine white tiles. They folded them neatly and piled them up, like nightmarish shop assistants. I tried not to look at Effie, who sat there, looking terribly concerned. I wondered what she thought when she saw the scarred and mangled hotch-potch of my naked form. A form I was usually deadset on hiding from everyone: from the whole world.

What had got into me tonight? Why didn't I care?

Effie made worried noises as I stepped inside the gleaming chrome coffin-shaped machine. It was like climbing inside a vast bread-maker. I ignored her protests and let the little women close the door on me.

The silence and dark lasted a few moments, and then the treatments began.

This is what Jessie had gone through. This is what all the women of the town were signing up to undergo. This is what had panicked Effie and made her push her way out. It didn't seem so bad to me. A few pulsing, flashing, multi-coloured lights. Weird, ululating noises; a curious vibration, as if every molecule of my body was being set free to bounce about in the enclosed space. And, just as Effie had said: the sensation of lots of tiny hands pummelling and pulling at each portion of my form: stretching and moulding me like dough...

The Deadly Machine was supposed to roll back the years. It was supposed to smooth your furrowed brow and ease all the tensions from your clapped-out body. You were meant to step out of it rejuvenated: all those years and the evidence of those years were supposed to be leached out of you. Effie had described it as being bled, or having life drained out of you by a vampire's kiss.

To me, it felt even more cataclysmic. Whatever it was that the machine did, reacted very strongly with my – shall we say, unique? – physicality. Lightning flashed and crashed inside the enclosed space. I was jerked about like a puppet and an awful smell of burning filled my nose.

I was running across the moors; ragged and bleeding, pursued by hounds... I was begging in an underpass, frozen with rain... I was living in a tower in a grand mansion, having been taken in... I was being shown the door, disgraced... I was standing on my father's doorstep and he stared at me in horror. His smart visitors and his wife were calling from the drawing room: 'But who is it?'... I was walking through the zoo and children were screaming... I was lying on an operating table... I was opening my eyes. The first thing I saw was the face of my husband, leering down at me, from a window high up in the stone wall. His face was twisted in a mixture of rage and desire...

How far back was this machine taking me? How much further back was there left?

Flashbacks! I was glimpsing moments from my past. And not the best ones. Just the most hair-raising. Just the most stressful. What was the machine doing? Taking me back through my long, phantasmagorical existence, through a series of snapshots I had tried so hard to block out of my mind...

My hands were playing the yellowish keys of a concert piano.

My breasts were suckling infants.

In some squalid alleyway, my throat was being slit.

Too many memories. Each part of my body has its own memory. Its own favourite moments. Each part of my body relived its own past, so that the different lifetimes overlapped; whizzing around inside my head. They reached a frenzied pitch and I screamed at the top of my voice. My voice seemed like a compound of a hundred different women's voices. I was a crowd. I was Legion: howling in dismay and a ghastly sense of loss inside the machine.

Everything I'd deliberately forgotten, and everything I'd only half-known, came flooding back to me in those moments.

It was too much for the machine.

There was an almighty crack. It was the noise of Excalibur coming free of its stone. Or the noise of the tree where Robin of Loxley hid out, crashing down after a thousand years in Sherwood. It was the noise of Prometheus being set free from his rock. And the sound of the lightning striking the conductors on the ramparts of Herr Doctor's castle...

It was a huge noise, that robbed me of my hearing for several minutes.

When I was pitched back into the immaculate laboratory, acrid smoke was billowing everywhere. I fell into Effie's arms though, of course, she wasn't strong enough to hold me. The assistants were squealing, though I couldn't hear a thing. I couldn't even hear The Deadly Machine's final wail of despair. I felt the reverberations, though, as it shuddered and died and eventually it was still.

'My god, woman,' Effie mouthed, crouching beside me on the floor. 'What did you do to it?'

She brought me my clothes and draped them over me. I felt like a huge baby, swaddled there, foetal, understanding nothing. When my hearing started to come back, I realised that Effie was saying: 'We need to get out of here. We need to leave right now.'

She was speaking in a low, urgent voice. I was suddenly more aware of what was going on around me, having supressed the lurid images in my head.

Mr Danby had lost his composure. No more the purring, composed little man. He was standing before his smashed, still smoking machine and screeching. He beat his fists against his temples and gnashed his teeth. He stamped his feet and swung round to face us. Unfortunate, as Effie was helping me to dress myself just at that moment. It wasn't the most elegant confrontation of my life.

'You have ruined us!' Mr Danby shrieked. 'You have destroyed everything.'

Effie kept her voice calm and low. 'Ignore him. Let's just get you sorted and get out of here.'

'The machine will never work again! You have spoiled it for everyone!'

At this, the overalled monkey women started to moan and pound their own temples with their tiny fists.

'You could have killed her,' Effie shouted back at him. 'I thought my ordeal was bad enough. But look at her! You could have murdered her!'

'There was nothing wrong with my machine,' he protested. 'Whatever happened is down to her. She sabotaged it somehow..!'

I stammered out a few words: 'It couldn't... cope with me... Couldn't regress me...' I had a shocking headache and my extremities were all numb. Other than that, I wasn't feeling as bad as all that by now.

'She's a freak!' Mr Danby yelled. 'A monster!'

'Hie!' Effie cried. 'Don't you say things like that about my friend.' Leaving me to finish dressing, she stormed over to confront the little man. His assistants leaped to protect him. All of them seemed wary of Effie. She was wiry and determined. She could have given them all a good thrashing and, after last time, they looked like they knew it.

'You don't understand what you've done,' Mr Danby sighed. His whole body sagged. 'This machine... these treatments... they didn't hurt anyone. They couldn't. What we did here was for the benefit of all womankind.'

The monkey women chattered excitedly, agreeing with him.

'And these women?' Effie said. 'Are these indebted to your machine, too?'

'Hm?' he asked. 'Well, yes. They are. Not every patient regressed as far as my assistants. Not everyone would choose to go that far...'

'My god,' Effie hissed. 'You're insane! Who'd want to be like that? Is this what's happening to Jessie? Shrinking and wrinkling up? You've turned her into a neanderthal woman?'

'Australopithecus, actually,' he said. 'It sometimes happens. It isn't supposed to.'

I was fit and decent enough, by now, to join in their conversation. 'But why?' I demanded. 'Why bother? What do you get out of it? What makes you want to go round regressing women?'

'Time,' he said sadly. 'What my machine drew out of them was time itself. I was siphoning the very distillation of their remaining years out of their cells and their veins. Oh, not in a way that would harm them.

Indeed, mostly, it improved them. And I got to *bottle* time itself. The gorgeous, viscous juice of time.'

And at that point we noticed the glass jars on the shelves on the far wall. Red and blue with thick liquids.

'He's crazy,' Effie hissed. 'You can't *bottle* time...'

'Oh, I could,' Mr Danby sighed. 'That's precisely what I did. And now you've spoiled it all. You've spoiled everything.'

'But what did you want it for? What are you doing with that stuff?' I asked.

'Upstairs in this house lies my mother,' he said, sadly. 'She is very, very old. Older even than you, Brenda. But her time now is short. She is a very special, very great person, you see and I have been trying to buy her a little longer...'

'By stealing years and months from innocent women,' Effie accused him. 'You're like Jack the Ripper!'

'Hardly,' he shrugged. 'Nobody lost out. Not really. Those women have only awful, lonely decrepitude waiting for them. Who really wants to be old and worn out and burdensome? My machine squeezes and pulverizes the very cells of their exhausted bodies, wringing out the last vestiges of energy and transforming it into that wonderful, syrupy elixir. All my ladies have lost is but the cumbersome years of their decline. Now they are regressed and they get to enjoy one last glorious burst of rejuvenation. And so, yes... I stole their time away, technically... but wasn't it just wasted time? Time when they would be past it?'

Effie and I exchanged a quick, horrified glance. The madman ranted on:

'Now you see the glory of my plan! You *do* see, don't you? I steal their liquid essence, these delightful ladies, and I bottle it and stopper it up for my dear old mother and, in turn, I give my clientele one last golden swansong... but I do it only because they asked. And they keep asking me. They all want to have a make-over from me. It is a very neat arrangement.'

'It's vile,' Effie said, through gritted teeth. 'And all for some... vampire hag in your attic?'

'Mother will be so very disappointed,' he sighed. 'She will be have to be told who has caused this disaster. Someone will have to pay.' He clicked his fingers wearily. 'Seize them, would you?'

We realised that, in his own mild way, he was commanding his simian assistants to attack us.

They weren't quite so mild and polite as their master. He ducked away and left them to it, as the little women snarled and bared their pointed teeth at us. They advanced with shuffling steps. Effie and I drew away from them, back to back, as if preparing for fisticuffs in a brawl.

'This is ridiculous!' Effie cried. 'Saturday night and we're having a fight in a mad scientist's laboratory!' She sounded almost gleeful. One of the monkey women launched herself at Effie then and was knocked back by a quick slap in the chops. As I'd suspected, Effie could be quite useful in a punch-up.

Soon, all fifteen, twenty, thirty of the Australopithe-cus women were hurling themselves at us. Tiny arms and legs were flashing out and we were being pummelled and punched from all angles.

'Where's Danby gone?' grunted Effie, as she whirled into action with her recently-acquired jujitsu. The women shrank back, horrified at this sexagenarian dervish.

'He's fled!' I cried. 'Probably gone to explain himself to his dear old mamma.'

Effie grunted again, as she flung one marsupial-like woman at a huddle of her companions. 'Then I suggest we get out of here, the back way, and make good our escape.'

I waded through the attacking bodies, using every iota of my not inconsiderable strength. These women were indefatigable though and determined to keep us captive. But we were determined too: we weren't staying in The Deadly Boutique a moment longer.

'Shouldn't we go upstairs and sort his mother out?' I asked Effie, as we reached the metal outer door.

'Sort her out?'

'Stake her through the heart, or whatever,' I suggested. 'So they don't start up again!'

'Stake her through the heart?' With one hand Effie was struggling with locks and bolts. With the other she was helping me hold the little women back. 'My god, Brenda. This is Whitby! We don't go staking people through the heart!'

At that moment the metal door sprang open, revealing the chill mist of the backyard and alleyways beyond.

'Will they follow us?'

But we didn't even turn round to look. Effie and I grasped each other's hands and pelted out into the freezing night. We tore into the narrow alleys, twisting and turning and heading for home.

We had to stop for a moment, to catch our breath. We clutched our knees, breathing raggedly, pausing outside Woolworths. 'Have we lost them?'

There came no slap-slap-slap of tiny feet in pursuit. There was nothing. Silence.

Town was eerily silent tonight. We were back in the town centre, outside ordinary shops. It felt weird, even thinking about being chased by regressed monkey women; or about a man who bottled time in order to feed it to his ailing mother upstairs.

'What have we been involved in?' Effie asked hollowly. 'What kind of madness was that?'

'An adventure!' I grinned. Suddenly, I had to ask her the thing that had been bugging me, ever since The Deadly Machine had its nervous breakdown and exploded with me still inside it. 'So... did it work on me? Did it transform me?'

'Hm?'

'The Machine!' I said, as we set off again; not running this time, but walking at quite a clip, through the warren of streets towards home. 'Has it made me younger? Will I knock them dead?'

'Oh, erm,' said Effie. 'I can't really tell in this light. The street lamps are too harsh. Maybe it has, maybe it hasn't worked. I'm not sure.'

I chuckled at her evasiveness as we set off up the hill towards our houses.

'Do you *feel* any different?' Effie asked me.

'Oh, yes,' I said, breathing deeply, and realising how true that was. 'Do you know, for the first time in ages... I feel *alive.*'

The End.